DINK, JOSH, AND RU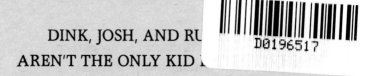
AREN'T THE ONLY KID :

WHAT ABOUT YOU?

Can you find the hidden message inside this book?

There are 26 illustrations in this book, not counting the one on the title page, the map at the beginning, or the picture of the White House that repeats at the start of many of the chapters. In each of the 26 illustrations, there's a hidden letter. If you can find all the letters, you will spell out a secret message!

If you're stumped, the answer is on the bottom of page 131.

HAPPY DETECTING!

This book is dedicated to my parents,
who gave me my first book.
—R.R.

To Zebediah Metlei Frederick Knapp and Augustus Flapjack
—J.S.G.

Text copyright © 2008 by Ron Roy
Cover art copyright © 2015 by Stephen Gilpin
Interior illustrations copyright © 2008 by John Steven Gurney

All rights reserved. Published in the United States by Random House Children's Books, a division of Random House LLC, a Penguin Random House Company, New York. Originally published in paperback by Random House Children's Books, New York, in 2008.

Random House and the colophon and A to Z Mysteries are registered trademarks and A Stepping Stone Book and the colophon and the A to Z Mysteries colophon are trademarks of Random House LLC.

Visit us on the Web!
SteppingStonesBooks.com
randomhousekids.com

Educators and librarians, for a variety of teaching tools, visit us at RHTeachersLibrarians.com

Library of Congress Cataloging-in-Publication Data
Roy, Ron.
White House white-out / by Ron Roy ; illustrated by John Steven Gurney.
p. cm. — (A to Z mysteries Super edition ; #3) "A Stepping Stone Book."
Summary: When Dink, Josh, and Ruth Rose visit Washington, D.C., just before Christmas, they are inadvertently caught up in a kidnapping plot that was intended for the president's dog, but also involves the president's stepdaughter and her friend Marshall.
ISBN 978-0-375-84721-9 (trade) — ISBN 978-0-375-94721-6 (lib. bdg.) —
ISBN 978-0-307-47783-5 (ebook)
[1. Kidnapping—Fiction. 2. Dogs—Fiction. 3. Washington (D.C.)—Fiction. 4. Virginia—Fiction. 5. Mystery and detective stories.] I. Gurney, John Steven, ill. II. Title. III. Series: Roy, Ron.
A to Z mysteries Super edition ; #3.
PZ7.R8139 We 2008 [Fic]—dc22 2007031560
Printed in the United States of America
22 21

This book has been officially leveled by using the F&P Text Level Gradient™ Leveling System.

Random House Children's Books supports the First Amendment and celebrates the right to read.

A to Z Mysteries®

SUPER EDITION 3

White House White-out

by **Ron Roy**

illustrated by
John Steven Gurney

A STEPPING STONE BOOK™

Random House 🏠 New York

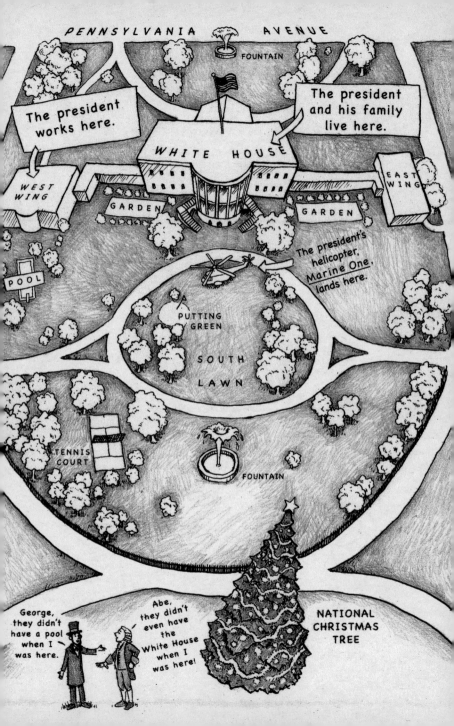

CHAPTER 1

Josh stuck out his tongue into the cold December air.

"What are you doing?" Ruth Rose asked him.

"Trying to catch snowflakes," Josh said. "I'm hungry."

Dink laughed at his friend. "You'll freeze your tongue off," he said. Dink's full name was Donald David Duncan, but his friends called him Dink.

Josh looked at his two best friends through the falling snow. "Really?"

Ruth Rose nodded. She liked to dress all in one color, a different color each day. Today it was red, from her boots to her gloves to her knitted cap.

"Bummer," Josh said.

The kids were in Washington, D.C. It was the week before Christmas, and they had taken the train from Connecticut with Dink's father. While the kids were sightseeing, he would be doing research in the Library of Congress. Dink, Josh, and Ruth Rose had visited the National Zoo first and had just left the Washington Monument.

"How much farther to the White House?" Josh asked as they trudged through the snow. It was six inches deep, covering the sidewalks, lawns, and most of their boots.

Ruth Rose pulled out her guide to Washington, D.C. She opened to a map of the city. "We're right here, on Seventeenth Street," she said. They were headed toward their hotel on K Street.

"Here's the White House," Dink said. He put a gloved finger on the map. "Only a few more blocks."

"And there's our hotel," Ruth Rose said, moving her finger on the map. "It's only a little way past the White House."

"When we get back, I'm having steak for supper," Josh announced. "With a mountain of mashed potatoes and a giant piece of chocolate cake for dessert."

Dink rolled his eyes.

"Look, there's the National Christmas Tree!" Ruth Rose said. She pointed to the right. Through the falling snow, they could make out the tall tree. Its thousands of Christmas lights glowed like jewels through the dim, snowy afternoon.

"Wow!" Josh said. "That must be the tallest Christmas tree in the world! Let's go see it."

They turned right and walked about two hundred yards to the base of the tree. A few tourists were there taking pictures. A couple of little kids were trying to build a snowman.

"Guys, look," Dink said.

Josh and Ruth Rose turned around and followed Dink's gaze. Only a few hundred yards away stood the White House. Even through falling snow, the building was easy to see. The front was surrounded by a curve of black fence. Lights shone through dozens of windows.

"Gosh, it's so . . . white," Josh said.

"It's the oldest public building in D.C.," Ruth Rose said.

"I heard Lincoln's ghost walks around inside," Josh said.

Ruth Rose grinned. "Ooooh, Josh believes in ghosts," she said.

"I wish we had time for a tour," Dink said. He looked at his watch. "It's four-thirty and I told Dad we'd be at the hotel by five."

Ruth Rose consulted her book again. "The next tour is tomorrow at noon," she informed the boys.

The kids hiked through the snow toward the White House. They stopped at the tall black fence and stared through the iron bars.

Ruth Rose opened her guidebook again. She read a paragraph:

"President Zachary Thornton and First Lady Lois Corcoran Thornton are the White House's current residents. They share the White House with the First Lady's daughter, Katherine, and their many pets."

"Wow, it must be awesome to live in the White House," Josh said. He put his face up against the fence. "Think of all the rooms you could play hide-and-seek in!"

"How many rooms are there?" Dink asked Ruth Rose.

Ruth Rose looked in her book. "One hundred and thirty-two," she said. "But most of them aren't open to the public."

Just then a dog came bounding through the snow inside the fence. The dog was tall and gray, with long, skinny legs. It was wearing a red sweater with cutouts for the legs and tail.

A boy and girl about the same age as Dink raced after it, both covered with snow. They saw Dink, Josh, and Ruth Rose looking through the fence.

Their dog trotted over and stuck its snout between the rails.

Dink noticed some words stitched in white on the dog's red sweater. The words said FIRST DOG.

"Is your dog friendly?" Dink asked the two kids.

"Sure," the girl said. "Natasha is a greyhound, and she loves everyone!"

Dink noticed red hair sticking out from under the girl's hat.

Dink, Josh, and Ruth Rose took off their gloves. They put their hands through the fence bars and patted the dog's sleek head.

"My name is KC," the girl said. "This is my friend Marshall. We're trying to teach Natasha a Christmas trick. But she doesn't like the snow, so she's trying to escape."

"I'm Dink Duncan, and these are my friends Josh and Ruth Rose," Dink said. "We're here with my dad. We live in Connecticut."

The five kids all shook hands through the fence. All the hands made it confusing, and they burst out laughing.

"Are you the president's daughter?" Josh asked KC.

"Nope, I'm his stepdaughter," KC said. "He and my mom got married last year."

"Sweet!" Josh said. "So what's it like living in the White House? Do you get to do any cool stuff?"

"She gets to do anything she wants!" Marshall piped up.

KC poked Marshall. She looked through the fence at Dink, Josh, and Ruth Rose. "Would you like to come in?"

Dink gulped. "In there?" he asked. "In the White House?"

KC grinned. "Sure. My folks aren't home, but I know they wouldn't mind," she said. "I just have to get you clearance."

"Wicked!" Josh yelled.

Ruth Rose laughed. "Just hide your food," she told KC. "Josh will eat anything."

Dink glanced at his watch. "Um, we

can't stay long," he said. "My dad's expecting us back at our hotel in a half hour."

"Which hotel?" KC asked.

"It's the Royal Grove on Sixteenth Street," Ruth Rose said. "That's not far, right?"

"Nope, just a couple of blocks behind the White House," KC said. "You'll make it in plenty of time."

"So how do we get clearance?" Josh asked.

"Go around to the next gate," KC said, pointing to the right. "We'll meet you there with one of the marine guards. He'll give you special passes."

"That'll be great," Dink said. "Wait'll I tell my dad!"

Dink, Josh, and Ruth Rose raced each other to the next gate. They stood there, peering inside as snowflakes covered their eyelashes.

Finally they saw KC, Marshall, and Natasha coming toward them through the snow. With them was a tall marine. He wore shiny black boots and a dark green uniform under a long coat. His hat and shoulders were white with snow-flakes.

The guard looked at the kids closely before he unlocked the gate. He handed them each a pass. "Please clip these onto your clothing," he said. He asked their names and wrote them on a clipboard. He also took down Dink's father's name and the name of the hotel. Then he said, "Welcome to the White House," and walked away toward a small guard hut.

"Okay, follow me," KC said. She led everyone to a rear door.

At least ten small trucks and vans were parked near the entrance. Each one had about six inches of snow on top, as if they'd been parked there for hours. Men and women wearing clearance badges pulled boxes from the vans and lugged them into the White House. Three men were sliding a Christmas tree out of one of the trucks.

"The White House is getting decorated today," KC explained. "When they're all done, the public gets to come in for tours."

"They have ten Christmas trees!" Marshall said. "And about a zillion wreaths. Wait'll you see!"

A woman carrying a green wreath stopped to pat Natasha on the head. Natasha licked her hand before KC led the kids into a hallway, where they hung their coats and hats. Dozens of people rushed around carrying wreaths, strings of lights, garlands of greenery, and armloads of ornaments. Dink loved the smell of pine, and it was everywhere.

KC led them along the hallway. They stepped over boxes and around the workers. Dink peeked into a room and saw a Christmas tree covered with white paper cranes.

In every window someone had hung a wreath. Red ribbon dangled from chandeliers. Golden plastic fruit that looked real lay in piles waiting to be arranged on tabletops. No matter where you looked, someone was decorating something.

"This is amazing!" Dink said as they walked through the confusion.

"I can't wait till they're all finished," KC whispered. "My mom and stepfather are getting our own little tree for upstairs. We're going to decorate it tonight after everyone else is gone."

"Tell them about your present for your stepdad," Marshall told KC.

KC peeked into a small room that

looked like an office. "Come on in here," she said to the rest of the kids.

The room had a soft carpet, and they all sat. "A few months ago, we adopted Natasha as a surprise for the president," KC said. "He's been trying to teach her tricks, but she won't listen to him. He's so funny! He says, 'Natasha, you have to listen, I'm the president!'"

Everyone laughed.

"So Marsh and I are trying to teach Natasha to sing when I blow a whistle," KC went on. "That will be my present to my stepfather."

KC pulled a silver whistle from her pocket. "It's silent to human ears," she said. "But dogs can hear it."

"Can you show us?" Josh asked. He looked around the room. "Where is Natasha, anyway?"

"Begging for food somewhere, probably," Marshall said.

"Just like Josh," Dink said.

KC blew on the whistle. When Natasha didn't show up, the kids went looking for her. They peeked into every room, asking the decorators if they'd noticed the dog anywhere.

No one had.

"Maybe she went outside again," Dink suggested.

KC shook her head. "She hates the snow," she said. "She only goes out when I take her."

"Why don't we split up and search?" Ruth Rose asked.

"Good idea," KC said. "Marsh, you take Dink and Josh and look down here. I'll check the upstairs with Ruth Rose. Meet back here in ten minutes in front of this clock, okay?"

Dink looked at his watch. They had to be back at the hotel in about twenty minutes. He glanced out one of the

windows. It was beginning to get dark.

The five kids split off to begin their search. They called the dog's name and asked everyone they saw, and KC blew on the whistle. Ten minutes later, they met under the clock.

No one had seen Natasha.

"She's nowhere," KC said. "I even went upstairs to our private rooms. I looked under all the beds, her usual spot to hide from us. How could a sixty-pound dog disappear?"

CHAPTER 2

Dink could tell that KC was upset. "Let's try looking outside," he suggested. "Maybe one of the decorator people accidentally locked her out."

"I guess it's worth a try," KC said.

The kids scrambled into their coats and headed into the snow. It was falling harder. Earlier the snowflakes had been large and fluffy, coming down softly. Now the flakes were small and were swept by a stiff wind. Dink had to squint his eyes to see through the stuff.

"Does anyone see her?" KC asked.

No one did.

Workers hurried back and forth, bringing in more things to make the White House look Christmassy.

All five kids called and whistled. Natasha did not come bounding through the snow as they all hoped she would.

Dink noticed a man scraping snow off the windshield of one of the trucks. "Wait a sec," Dink said to the others. He scuffed through the snow up to the man.

"Excuse me, have you seen a dog?" he asked. "She's gray and skinny."

The man turned. His nose and ears were red from the cold. "Over there, where the vans are parked near the fence," he said. "I saw a woman with a dog about ten minutes ago."

Dink told the other kids what he'd learned. They all raced through the parking area. Then KC began shouting Natasha's name. There was no answering bark.

"Look for footprints," Ruth Rose said.

Five pairs of eyes studied the snow-covered ground. What prints they saw were all made by human boots. Even these were quickly getting covered with fresh snow.

"Why don't you try your dog whistle?" Marshall suggested.

KC beamed at Marshall. "Why didn't I think of that?"

She put the whistle in her mouth and blew as hard as she could.

Dink and the others heard no sound.

"Are you sure that thing works?" Josh asked. "I mean, what if—"

"Shhh, I think I heard something," Ruth Rose said.

The five kids stood silently, listening as the snow fell softly around them. Dink heard only the wind and the hum of traffic.

KC tried the whistle again.

This time they all heard a dog howling.

"NATASHA!" KC yelled. "Come, girl! Come, girl!"

They heard more howling and barking.

"Maybe she's in one of these vans or trucks," Josh said.

"How could she be?" Marshall asked.

"Well, she's not coming," Ruth Rose said. "KC, who owns all these cars?"

"The people inside doing the decorating," KC said. "They pulled up to the door to unload their stuff, then they parked over here."

"Would Natasha jump inside someone's car?" Dink asked. "Maybe to get out of the snow?"

"I don't know," KC said.

"Keep using the dog whistle," Dink said. "And we can walk around and look in all the windows."

The kids split up and began wiping truck and van windows. KC kept blowing the whistle.

Dink approached a long white van. A sign on the side said FLOWERS BY JO. There were no rear windows, so Dink walked toward the front of the van. He called out Natasha's name loudly. Suddenly he heard a howl from inside. "Over here!" Dink cried. "I think I found her!"

The other four kids came running. They wiped off all the windows and tiptoed to peek inside.

"I don't see her in there," KC said. "NATASHA, ANSWER ME, GIRL!"

Excited barking came from inside the van.

"She's in there!" Dink said. "Try the doors, guys."

Both front doors were locked. But

when the kids tried the van's double rear doors, they opened.

Dink expected Natasha to leap out, but she didn't. The kids stared into the van's rear compartment. Three sides were lined with shelves holding florist supplies. Dink saw spools of ribbon and wire, tools, some plastic fruit, and a bunch of fake Christmas flowers. On the left near the doors, a spare tire stood, clamped to the wall.

Straight ahead of them, backed up against the driver's compartment, sat a large wooden crate. Someone had printed WHITE HOUSE WREATHS on the wood with a black marker. Several folded packing quilts were stacked on top of the crate.

"She's not here!" KC said.

"But we all heard her!" Marshall said. "She *has* to be!"

Then Natasha began barking again.

"She's in that crate!" Ruth Rose said.

They all scrambled into the back of the van, leaving the doors open a crack behind them. There were no windows, but a little light came through the rear doors.

Dink felt carpeting under his knees. His fingers felt pine needles, and the air smelled of them.

Suddenly a tiny light went on.

"What's that?" Josh asked.

"It's me," Ruth Rose said. "I have a light on my key chain."

Using the small glow, the kids examined the crate. They heard Natasha's nails scratching at the wood inside.

"I'm here, Natasha!" KC said into the crate.

"How the heck did she get in there, anyway?" Josh asked.

Dink and Josh swept the blankets off the top. KC tried to lift the lid.

"It's stuck!" she said.

"No, it's wired shut," Marshall said. "Someone put her in here on purpose!"

He and Dink worked together to untwist the wire. Then the crate lid was up and Natasha leaped out. Her red sweater was covered with pine needles.

KC wrapped her arms around Natasha while the dog licked her face and trembled. "Girl, what happened to you?" she asked.

Just then they heard the doors behind them slam shut. Except for Ruth Rose's tiny light, they were in total darkness.

"Who closed the doors?" Marshall whispered.

Before any of them could answer, the engine roared to life. Natasha began barking.

The kids were knocked off balance as the van suddenly backed up. Then

there was a sharp turn, and they fell
again as the van lurched forward.

"Where are we going?" Ruth Rose
whispered in the dark.

"We don't have to whisper. The driver can't hear us," Dink said. The wall that separated them from the front cab would absorb all sounds from the back.

"Guys, I think we're being kidnapped!" Josh said.

"But I don't think he knows we're back here," Marshall said. "The only windows are up in front. I'll bet he's trying to steal Natasha!"

"Maybe the kidnapper used Natasha as bait," Ruth Rose said.

"What do you mean?" Josh asked.

"To get KC in the van," Ruth Rose said.

"Why would some florist want me?" KC asked.

"For ransom," Ruth Rose said. "The president's stepdaughter is worth a lot of money."

CHAPTER 3

"She's right," Marshall said. "Your mom and President Thornton would pay anything to get you back."

KC didn't say anything. She sat on the carpeted floor and hugged Natasha. The other kids sat near her. It was cold in the van, so they spread the packing quilts over their legs.

The van roared on to no one knew where.

"What are we gonna do?" Marshall asked.

"I don't know," KC said. "My mom and the president probably aren't even home yet. They don't know we're gone."

Dink thought about his father waiting for him at the hotel. "Can I see your light?" he asked Ruth Rose.

He shone the tiny glow on his watch. It was five o'clock. "My dad doesn't know we went to the White House," he told the other kids. "When we don't show up at five, he'll call the cops."

"But how will the cops find us?" Josh asked. "They won't know where to look!"

"The president can get an airplane, right?" Marshall asked KC. "Or a helicopter?"

"But it's snowing, Marsh," KC said. "And we're in a white van. They'd never see us."

"Plus, it must be getting dark by now," Josh reminded them all.

"I wish we could see out," Marshall said.

"I wonder where he's planning on

taking us," Ruth Rose said.

"Somewhere there's food, I hope," Josh muttered.

Marshall giggled. "Maybe Jo'll stop for a burger," he said.

Josh chuckled in the dark. "Right. He'll go up to the counter and say, 'Five orders of burgers, fries, and shakes, please. Better wrap 'em to go. I'm kidnapping a bunch of kids.'"

The kids stopped talking. Dink could hear the van's loud engine. Beneath him, he felt the vibration and hum of moving tires. His stomach growled. "Thanks a lot, Josh," he said. "Now you made me hungry."

"At least we have these blankets," Josh said.

The van slowed, then made a turn. Dink could feel the difference. They had been humming along smoothly, and now the road seemed bumpier.

"I think we're on a back road now," he said to the others.

"If you drive out of downtown Washington, D.C.," KC said, "you can be in the country pretty fast. We could be well into Virginia by now."

The bumpy ride continued. The kids had to grab hold of the shelves to keep their balance.

Dink checked his watch every few minutes using Ruth Rose's penlight. "It's almost six o'clock," he told the others.

Suddenly the van swerved sharply to the right. It seemed to go over a huge bump. The kids were thrown into the air, then landed together in a pile. Then Dink felt another rough bump, and the kids were hurled toward the crate. They stopped suddenly with a sharp jolt. The floor of the van was at a crazy angle, as if they'd landed in a hole. Natasha was barking wildly.

"What the heck happened?" Josh asked. He was under Marshall.

"We've had an accident!" Dink said. "Listen, the motor stopped."

"Is everybody okay?" KC asked.

"I banged my arm," Josh said.

"How bad is it?" Dink asked.

"I don't know," Josh answered. "I don't think it's broken."

The kids untangled themselves. Ruth Rose turned on her light. "Is Natasha okay?" she asked.

"I think so," KC said. "She's licking my face."

"Josh, take the light and make sure your arm is all right," Ruth Rose said.

Josh aimed the small glow onto his arm. "No blood," he said.

"So we won't have to cut it off," Dink observed.

"Very amusing, Dinkus," Josh said. "I'm almost laughing."

They sat still, waiting to see if the van would start up again.

"Guys, what if the driver comes back here to check on Natasha?" Marshall said.

"If he does, we jump him!" Josh said. "If all five of us do it, he won't stand a chance!"

"Then what?" Dink asked. "What do we do with him?"

"We can tie him up like a Christmas present!" Marshall said. "I saw some wire on one of the shelves."

The kids waited. They sat awkwardly on the tilted floor. Dink expected to hear something or to see the van's rear doors open. Nothing happened. Dink heard only breathing and saw only darkness.

"This doesn't make sense," Ruth Rose said after a minute. "What could he be doing up there?"

"Do you think he just left?" Marshall asked. "He could've decided to try to get help."

"I didn't hear the driver's door open," Dink said. "But he could be hurt. Maybe he hit his head when we stopped."

"Oh my gosh, maybe he died!" Josh said. "We're trapped in the snow with a dead body!" He switched on Ruth Rose's light.

The kids looked at each other nervously. Dink told himself there was no way Josh could be right. "How could the driver have been killed?" he asked. "We didn't hear a crash, so he didn't hit a tree or another car."

"This is creepy. I'm getting out of here," Josh announced. He crawled uphill to the doors and tried the inside handle. "We're locked in!"

Marshall moved up next to Josh. "I saw this in a movie," he said. "We lie on our backs with our feet against the doors. Then we all kick the doors at the same time. Together we should be strong enough to bust the lock."

"Let's try it," Ruth Rose said. "We can't stay here forever!"

The kids lined up on their backs close to the doors.

"Everyone get ready," Josh said. "On three. One, two, THREE!"

Ten feet smashed against the doors. They flew open, letting a blast of snow and freezing air into the compartment.

The kids stared outside, squinting into the snow that flew into their faces. It was almost completely dark. There were no streetlights. Dink couldn't even see the road they'd been traveling on. But he did see a path of crushed snow that the van had plowed through.

Dink saw tall, dark shadows not far from the van. He figured they were trees.

Natasha began whimpering. KC hugged the dog, keeping a hand on her collar.

"Where the heck are we?" Josh asked.

"Out in the middle of nowhere," Marshall said.

"We should go check on the driver," Ruth Rose whispered.

"Wait! He could be dangerous!" Josh said. "What if he's got a gun!"

"Josh, he's a florist," Ruth Rose said.

"A florist who kidnaps dogs!" Josh insisted.

"Maybe he has a glue gun," Dink said with a giggle. He felt silly, and he knew it was because he was so scared.

KC jumped out into the snow. The other four kids followed. Wind howled out of the darkness, shooting stinging snow into their faces.

"Don't shut the doors," Josh said. "We don't want to get trapped outside."

Dink examined the lock. "This is busted," he said. He tried both handles. "See? It doesn't lock at all now."

"The snow is over my knees!" Ruth Rose said.

Dink looked around. Maybe they had crashed near a house, stores, anything. But he saw nothing but snow and darkness. His eyes were tearing and his nose felt like it might freeze.

"Come on," Dink said to the others.

KC left Natasha in the van, commanding her to stay.

The five kids struggled around to the driver's door. The van had plowed into a ravine. Its front end was buried in deep snow. The driver's door was buried, too.

Dink wiped the driver's window with his glove. He peered through the glass. The driver was slumped over the steering wheel. He wasn't moving.

CHAPTER 4

Josh put his face next to Dink's and looked inside the cab.

"Oh gosh, I see blood on his mouth," he said.

"We have to get this door open!" Dink said.

The kids kicked at the snow until they'd cleared space for the door to swing.

Dink grabbed the handle and turned. The door swung open. Dink felt a wave of warmth from the cab's heater. An empty coffee cup fell out of the cab.

The kids huddled around Dink and

looked at the driver. "Is he dead?" Marshall asked.

"It's a she, not a he," KC said. "That's lipstick, not blood. And I can see her breath. She's breathing."

The driver wore a white cap with a red pom-pom on top. She wore jeans that were tucked into tall, furry boots. Her red jacket was puffy.

"I saw her patting your dog when you took us inside the White House," Dink said to KC. "She was carrying a wreath."

The kids crowded around to get a look at the woman who had kidnapped Natasha. She looked like she was in her thirties, Dink thought. Strands of black hair showed at the edges of her hat.

"Look, she has a bump on her forehead," Ruth Rose said.

"Yuck, it's all purple," Josh added.

"She must have hit her head on the

steering wheel," Dink said.

"What should we do with her?" Marshall asked. "What if she wakes up?"

"We shouldn't move her," Dink said. "She might have a broken bone or something."

"But we can't just leave her here," Ruth Rose said. "It would be warmer with the rest of us in the van. And we could check on her to make sure she's okay."

"Maybe you're right," Dink said. He stretched across the driver and popped open the glove compartment. Under a bunch of papers, he spotted what he'd been hoping for. A flashlight. He grabbed it and slipped it into a pocket.

Then he looked through the papers until he found what he wanted. "Her name is Josephine Payne," Dink said, reading from one of the papers. "She lives on Q Street in Washington."

"If she lives in the city, why drive way out here in the country?" KC asked. "Why wouldn't she just bring Natasha to her house?"

"When she wakes up, we can ask her," Ruth Rose said.

"Can we carry her?" KC asked.

"With all of us helping, we can," Marshall said.

The five kids stamped on the snow, making a broad path from the driver's door to the rear doors.

Dink unsnapped the seat belt, and they dragged Jo Payne out of the cab. "Everybody grab an arm or leg!" he yelled.

"I've got her head," KC said.

Trying not to stumble on the uneven snow, they lugged the woman to the van's rear doors. It was a struggle, but they finally managed to shift her into the compartment. At one point, the woman let out a little moan.

"Cover her with some of these blankets!" Dink said. He flipped on the flashlight and shone it onto the pile they'd
left behind.

The kids sat together in a bunch. Natasha plopped herself across KC's legs. They watched Jo Payne, but the woman didn't move an eyelash.

Dink switched off the flashlight. He pulled off his gloves and stuck his hands under his armpits. "Anyone have an idea?" he asked. "It's getting colder and darker. It may be hours before anyone finds us."

He wanted to add "If they find us."

"Can you turn on that flashlight, Dink?" Josh asked. "I feel like I'm talking to ghosts."

"No," Dink said. "We might need it later. I don't want to run down the batteries."

"Maybe Jo has a cell phone," Ruth Rose said. "We should probably check her pockets."

There were two zippered pockets in Jo Payne's jacket, but neither held a

phone. Ruth Rose patted the pockets in the woman's jeans, but they were flat. No cell phone.

"Why don't we walk up to that road we were on and hitchhike?" Josh said.

"Josh, it's freezing cold," Dink said. "It might be hours before a car comes along. Besides, we can't just leave the driver here."

"Well, what if two of us went for help, and the rest stayed here?" Marshall suggested. "There might be a gas station around the corner. Or a restaurant."

"It's dark and the snow is too deep," Dink said. "You could get lost out there."

"I agree with Josh," Ruth Rose said. "Look, Dink, the road is just up that hill. If she was driving on it, other cars could, too. Maybe a snowplow will come along. If we stay here in the van, it would never see us."

Dink thought for a minute. There

was a possibility that a car would come along. "Okay," he said. "Let's all go up and see what's what."

Dink spread another blanket over Jo Payne. He patted his pocket to check that he had the flashlight. Then the kids clambered outside again.

Natasha whimpered.

"No, Natasha, you stay," KC said. "Stay with the lady."

"Maybe Natasha knows the lady tried to kidnap her," Marshall said.

KC shut the doors. Because of the busted lock, they didn't close tightly.

The snow was still falling, but it had not filled in the wide path made by the van when it left the road. The kids walked single file, trying to step into each other's boot prints. The hill was steep and they kept slipping.

Josh broke a branch and used it as a staff to help him get up the hill.

They stopped at the top, out of breath. Snow swirled into their faces, making them squint their eyes. A thick pine tree stood only a few feet from the road's edge. Its branches were clotted with snow.

"This is where she went off the road," Dink said. He pointed the flashlight at the snowbank where it had been flattened. They could barely see the van, down the hill about thirty yards away.

"If anyone drove by here, they'd never notice the van down there," Marshall said. "And it's getting covered in snow!"

"Guys, where's the road?" Josh asked.

"I think we're standing on it," Ruth Rose said.

"But there are no tire marks!" KC said. "The snow covered them already."

The road—if there was one beneath their feet—was flat and white, like a meadow.

"I don't think this road gets plowed," Dink said. He handed the flashlight to Ruth Rose. Then he got down on his knees and started digging through the snow. "Josh, give me your stick," he said.

Josh handed the branch to Dink, who used it to dig deeper. Finally he stopped. "This isn't paved," he said. "It's just an old dirt road. They probably don't even use it in the winter."

"Then why was she driving on it?" Marshall asked.

"Maybe she was taking Natasha someplace out here to hide her," KC said. "Maybe she knew she couldn't keep a dog in her apartment."

"So what do we do now?" Josh asked.

"I say we go back to the van and get some sleep," Dink said. "When it's light out tomorrow, we can figure out what to do."

"Stay here all night?" Josh exclaimed. "But we have to eat!"

"Josh, you won't starve," Ruth Rose said. She scooped up a mittenful of snow and ate it. "Yummy!"

"We don't have much choice," Dink

said. "I know my dad would have called the cops by now. They could get here any minute, guys."

"I agree," KC said. "And the president will have the army, navy, and marines all out looking for us. We just have to wait."

"Come on," Dink said. "Lead the way, Ruth Rose."

The kids stumbled back down the steep hill. Ruth Rose and KC pulled open the van's rear doors. The boys were right behind them.

Suddenly KC cried, "Natasha is gone!"

CHAPTER 5

All five kids stared into the rear of the van. The mound of blankets covering Jo Payne was still there, exactly as Dink had left them.

"Where could Natasha be?" KC cried. "She was right here a minute ago!"

"Maybe she had to go out to, you know, do her thing," Marshall said.

"But where is she?" KC asked. "She'd stay near the van, Marsh."

"Maybe she pushed the door open and came looking for us," Ruth Rose said.

"But she'd have found us," KC insisted. "We weren't that far away!"

"Wait a minute," Josh said. He climbed into the van and crawled on his hands and knees to the other end. "Guys, Jo Payne is gone, too!" He tossed the blankets aside to prove his point.

"Maybe she took Natasha!" KC cried. "Oh, why did I leave them alone together?"

"But she was unconscious," Marshall said.

"Or faking it!" Ruth Rose said.

Dink stared at the pile of blankets. "She must have slipped out when we were up by the road," he said.

"But where would she go?" Josh asked. "It's not like she could call a cab and go back to D.C."

"Guys, there must be a reason why she drove way out here on this dirt road," Ruth Rose said. "What if she has a friend who lives near here? Maybe that's where she was taking Natasha when she had the accident. She must have regained consciousness when we moved her. Then, while we were outside, she grabbed Natasha and took off."

"Would Natasha go with her?" Dink asked KC.

"She might, especially if the woman had any food in her pockets," KC said. "Natasha would follow anyone for a treat."

"But just because they're both gone doesn't mean the woman took Natasha," Marshall said. "Maybe Jo Payne woke up and decided to take off while she had a chance. If she left the doors open, Natasha could have escaped that way."

"But why would she leave Natasha in the van after she went through all this trouble to steal her?" Josh asked. "I think she took Natasha with her."

"Marshall's right," Dink said. "They are both gone, but we don't know if they're together."

"Will you help me look for Natasha?" KC asked.

"Sure," Ruth Rose said. She closed the doors again.

The snow pelted their faces as they peered into the darkness. The wind made their eyes tear.

"NATASHA!" they all called over and over into the night. There was no returning bark. Natasha didn't come bounding through the snow.

"Try using your whistle," Ruth Rose suggested to KC.

KC blew on the dog whistle, but still no dog appeared.

"She'll freeze!" KC wailed.

"Dogs are descended from wolves," Josh said. "They know how to take care of themselves."

"Maybe she went for help," Ruth Rose suggested. "She might have run back to the White House."

"But that's miles away!" KC said.

"I saw a dog on TV who walked all the way across the country to get back home," Marshall said. "Natasha is pretty smart, KC. And don't forget, she's wearing that sweater your mom knitted."

"Hey, what's that?" Dink said. "I see lights over there!"

The kids turned and looked to where Dink was pointing. The glow of moving lights could be seen through the snow and darkness.

"What are they?" Marshall asked. "Could they be cars? Is that a road up there?"

Dink shook his head. "No, they're too slow, and the lights don't look bright enough for cars," he said.

"I'll bet they're snowmobiles!" Josh

said. He began jumping and waving. "Hey, snowmobiles! Yo, look over here!"

The other kids began to yell, too.

Dink turned on the flashlight and waved it over his head.

The lights continued moving, but they didn't come any closer.

"Wait a sec!" Josh said. He leaped for the driver's door and flung it open. He leaned in and pressed the horn on the steering wheel. Dink and the others heard a muffled sound. It wasn't nearly strong enough to carry through the night. The lights they'd seen might be a mile away.

Dink continued to wave the flashlight over his head. He screamed until his throat hurt.

Then the lights were gone. The kids stared at the spot where they'd seen them, but it was all blackness again.

"Maybe they saw us," Marshall said.

"Maybe they went for help."

Dink knew Marshall was just trying to make everyone feel better. "Yeah," he said. "For all we know, we're right next to a town."

"I have an idea," Marshall said. "The keys are still in the ignition. Why don't we start the motor? Maybe we can get the van out of the snowbank and drive away!"

"Marsh, you don't know how to drive," KC said.

"How hard can it be?" Marshall asked.

"I know how," Josh said. "My dad taught me. I drive our tractor all the time." He slid into the driver's seat and turned the key. The van shuddered once, then went still. Josh tried again. They all heard a ticking sound.

"Josh, even if you could start it up, the van is tilted," Dink said. "You'd need

a crane to pull it out of the snow."

Josh turned the key again. This time they heard nothing from the van's motor.

"It was a good idea, anyway," Dink told Marshall and Josh. "Come on, let's get back inside. My nose feels like an ice cube."

The kids climbed into the back of the van and huddled together. They covered up with the quilted blankets.

KC began to cry. "I miss Natasha," she said. "She always sleeps next to me."

The others tried to comfort KC, but she kept on sobbing.

"You know," Marshall said after a few minutes, "Natasha would hate to see you crying. She'd bark at you until you stopped."

KC sniffed. "You're right," she said. "Okay, no more crying."

"We need some entertainment," Josh

declared. "I'll sing to you! *'Dashing through the snow, in a—'*"

"Josh, shut up!" everyone yelled at the same time.

Dink smiled in the dark. Josh had a terrible singing voice, but at least KC wasn't crying anymore.

"Do you want to be a singer when you grow up?" KC asked Josh.

Dink figured she was trying to get her mind off her dog.

"No," Josh said. "I'm gonna be a chef in a restaurant in Hawaii. That way I can surf and cook at the same time."

"Good, we can all come and visit you and get free food," Dink said. "How about you, KC?"

"TV anchorwoman," KC said. "But I'll stay here in Washington, D.C., where the action is."

Dink told the others he wanted to be a writer, and Ruth Rose announced that

she was going to be the first woman president.

"Cool," KC said. "I'll only say nice things about you on TV." She nudged Marshall. "Tell them what you want to be, Marsh."

"A vet," he said. "But I'll take care of strange animals, not just cats and dogs."

"How strange?" Dink asked. "I mean, if Josh got sick, could we take him to you?"

"Ha-ha," Josh muttered.

"No," Marshall said. "It would be spiders, snakes, frogs, animals most people don't care—"

"Guys, I heard something!" Ruth Rose exclaimed. "It sounded like an airplane!"

CHAPTER 6

The five kids got up on their knees and listened.

"There it is again!" Ruth Rose said. "Hear it?"

"I do!" KC said.

"We're rescued!" Josh crowed.

All five kids scrambled out the door. Dink turned on the flashlight and began waving it toward the sky.

They stood in a circle, looking up and listening.

Nothing.

"I know I heard it," KC said.

"Maybe it'll come back," Dink said.

He shut off the flashlight.

Wind blew snow into their faces. Their boots made squeaking noises on the frozen snow.

"There it is again!" KC said.

"I hear it!" Dink said, switching the flashlight back on. "It sounds like a helicopter!"

"I hear it, too!" Ruth Rose said.

Then they all heard it. But Marshall was the first to see it. "Over there!" he yelled.

They all saw tiny blinking lights moving across the sky. They might have been fireflies except for the *thud-thud* of blades.

"It *is* a helicopter!" KC said. "It's the president looking for us!"

"Do you think they can see us?" KC asked.

"I don't know," Dink said. He waved the light wildly over his head.

"We need more light!" Josh said. "Let's make a bonfire!"

"With what?" Dink asked. "And we don't have any matches."

"Look inside the van," Marshall suggested. "Some of that florist stuff should burn."

"Guys, we need matches," Dink said again.

Josh raced to the van's passenger door and tore it open. He found some papers Dink had left on the seat.

"Any matches in there?" Dink asked.

"No, but there is a cigarette lighter," Josh said. He punched it in and waited, then it popped out. "It works!"

"Why don't we burn that wooden crate?" KC suggested. "We could break it apart!"

The kids worked frantically. They tugged the crate out the van's rear door. Dink grabbed some tools from a shelf,

and they were able to smash the crate into boards.

"Kick some snow into a big circle," Dink said.

When that was done, Josh lit a few of the papers. They threw on some decorations from inside the van. They added splinters, then small boards, from the crate. Soon they had a bonfire that lit

up the area behind the van.

"Now just come back, helicopter," Josh said.

The kids waited, warmed by the fire. No one spoke. Everyone was watching the black sky. Ashes flew upward, melting the snowflakes.

"Wait, what's that?" Ruth Rose asked, pointing.

"A star," Dink said. "It's not moving."

Josh dragged blankets from inside the van, and they all sat. Dink felt his face warm up.

Ten minutes went by without another sound from the sky.

"Be nice to have a few s'mores," Marshall commented.

"Be nice to have one huge marshmallow," Josh said.

"You'd have to share it five ways," Ruth Rose said.

Dink added more wood to the fire.

He was sure the orange and yellow flames could be seen from miles away, if anyone in a helicopter was looking down. If there even *was* a helicopter.

Josh tossed the last few boards onto the bonfire. "We're out of wood. I wonder if there are any dead tree branches around here," he said.

"I think we're surrounded by woods," Dink said. "But I'm not going looking in the dark."

"We need something that will burn for a long time," KC said. She looked around. The van's rear doors had been left open. "The spare tire!"

"Will that burn?" Marshall asked.

"Yes, it's rubber. It'll make black smoke!" Josh said.

In a minute, they had dragged the tire out of the van. Josh and KC rolled it onto the fire. The rubber caught fire, and soon dark smoke and flames were billowing up into the sky.

But the new fire smelled so bad the kids were forced to move their blankets twenty feet away. Right away their warm faces felt chilled.

The fire roared for a while, then settled into hissing and crackling. No one saw or heard the helicopter again.

"Guys, we should go inside and sleep," Dink suggested. "If a helicopter flies over, they'll see the fire."

Nobody wanted to give up, but they were all freezing. They grabbed the blankets and crawled into the van. Josh pulled the doors closed as tightly as he could. He wound some string around the handles to keep the cold out.

Now that the spare tire and crate were gone, there was room to stretch out. Dink kept the flashlight on only long enough for everyone to get settled.

"You know, if we weren't lost and

freezing and starving to death, this would be fun," Josh said.

Dink laughed out loud, but inside he wanted to cry. His father would be sick with worry.

"Good night, you guys," Dink said.

Dink dreamed about Christmas morning back home in Green Lawn, Connecticut. He saw their tree and the presents beneath it. One gift for his mom, one for his dad. But none of the presents had Dink's name on it.

He sat up with his heart thumping faster than normal. Where was he? Then he felt the lump of Josh's body next to his and he remembered.

It felt like a nightmare, but he knew it was all real. He, Josh, and Ruth Rose were trapped in a snowbank in the middle of nowhere with the president's stepdaughter and her friend. Her dog had disappeared out in the cold. No one knew where they were.

Dink shook his head to clear away the depressing thoughts. He tossed his blanket over Josh and crawled toward the van's rear doors. Everyone was fast asleep as he unwound the string Josh had used to keep the doors closed. He pushed them open and peeked out.

The fire was just red ashes now. The tire was completely burned, leaving the metal rim charred and black. At least it had stopped snowing.

Dink hopped to the ground and closed the doors behind him. He stretched and looked up. The sky was clear. Dink smiled when he saw the moon. Its glow lit the snow all around him.

Dink walked closer to the fire and checked his watch. It was nearly ten-thirty. Why did it feel like they'd been

stuck out here for much longer?

Firewood, he thought. *Got to get this fire blazing again.* He knew people were out looking for them and the fire would lead them here. He turned toward the black ring of trees around the clearing where the van had landed. No way was he going there.

Instead, Dink headed toward the road, remembering that he'd seen a small grove of trees there.

He crunched over the snow, sinking almost knee-deep with each step. Josh was right: this could be fun if it weren't so awful.

He reached the trees and got down on his knees to break off some of the lower branches. He heard something and looked up between two thick branches. Shadows were moving along the road. Behind the shadows came two people with the moon low behind them.

They were walking along the road, heading in his direction.

Dink almost stood up, but then he recognized something about the smaller figure. It was Jo Payne's hat: white with a red ball on top.

Dink shrank down into the snow, like a rabbit hiding from a fox. Jo Payne and her tall companion were twenty feet away and coming closer. Dink wriggled deep into the snow and prayed they wouldn't look into the trees.

The two stopped where the van had gone off the road.

"Happened right here," Jo Payne whispered. "It was like I was on ice. The next thing I remember was waking up in the back of my van with a headache. There were blankets over me. That was when I realized I had driven off with a bunch of kids along with the dog."

The other person grunted, then Dink saw him pull off his gloves and light a cigarette. He tossed the match into the snow. Ten feet away, Dink smelled the smoke.

"I heard the kids talking," Jo Payne went on. "When they all left, I made a leash for the dog and got the heck out of there."

"How'd you manage to let the dog get away?" the man asked.

"Ace, I didn't let it get away," Jo Payne answered. "How was I supposed to know that thing could chew through rope?"

The man coughed. "Well, it'll be dead by morning. I heard the howling again last night," he said. "The dog will be no match for a pack of hungry coyotes."

Coyotes! Dink squeezed his eyes shut. He tried to remember what he'd seen on TV about coyotes. Did they eat people?

"I never meant to harm the president's dog," the woman said. "I just wanted the money."

"Don't sweat over the dog," the man said. "The new plan will bring more money. We've got the president's daughter!"

He pulled two ski masks from a pocket and handed one to Jo. "Here, put this on," he ordered. "They'll all be asleep. You grab the girl, since you know what she looks like. I'll tie up the others."

"Where will we hide her?" the woman asked. "We can't put her in your cabin. By morning, there will be cops and FBI and who knows what else searching all over this valley."

Dink felt himself shivering. His teeth chattered so loud he was sure the two kidnappers would hear him. He was freezing, but he couldn't move.

"That old hunting shack by the pond behind my cabin," the man said. "No one knows it's there. It's in some trees. Can't even see it from my windows. A perfect place for the kid."

"What about the other four?" the woman asked.

"I don't know," the man said. "Let's just get the president's kid and worry about the other brats later."

"Ace, I don't like this plan," Jo Payne said.

"You got a better idea?" Ace asked.

"Yes," she said. "We go to your cabin and get your truck. We drive it back here, take the president's kid, blindfold the others. After we lock the girl in the shack, I'll stay there. You drive the other four back to Maple Crossing—it's only a couple of miles. There are phones there. They'll deliver our message to the president: two million for the kid. That's one million for each of us."

"Okay, I guess that makes sense," Ace said. "Then I'll bury the van in the snow with my plow. It'll be six months before anyone finds it." He laughed, coughed, and spit into the snow. "By then, we'll be far away and rich. Different names, maybe even different faces. Good-bye, Virginia. Hello, Mexico!"

The man flipped his cigarette. It landed two feet in front of Dink's face.

"Come on," the man said. "We got stuff to do."

Dink raised his head a few inches and watched the couple walk away.

Dink scuttled out of his hiding place. He found the half-smoked cigarette and put it in his pocket. Maybe Jo Payne's fingerprints would get wiped off the van, but Dink had the man's prints in his pocket!

CHAPTER 7

Dink plunged down the bank toward the van, tripping and falling every few feet. He leaped over the smoldering fire like an Olympic hurdler. He ripped the van doors open.

"Guys, wake up!" he yelled inside.

The lumps under the blankets moved.

"We have to get out of here!" Dink said as moonlight shone on four sleepy faces. "They're coming to get us!"

"I was dreaming about cheeseburgers," Josh said, blinking at Dink.

"Dream later!" Dink said. Then he told them about seeing Jo Payne and some guy a few minutes earlier. "She did take Natasha with her, but your dog chewed the rope, KC." He left out the part about coyotes prowling in the woods.

"Natasha got away?" KC said.

"Yeah," Dink said. "But now they want *you*! They're going to lock you in some shack and ask the president for two million dollars! We have to hide. They're coming back pretty soon!"

"Hide where?" Marshall asked.

"I don't know, anywhere," Dink said. "In the woods. Then after they bury the van, we can sneak back and dig our way into it."

"I have a better idea," KC said. "Let them put me in that shack. You four will get away, and you can tell the president where I am."

"No way!" Josh said. "We stick together."

"Josh is right," Ruth Rose said.

"Those people sound desperate. If we stay together, it's five against two."

"We're not leaving you," Dink said.

KC was outvoted. No way were her friends going to let her be stuck in a cold shack while they went home to hot chocolate and cookies.

"He said he's bringing his plow," Dink said. "When we hear it coming, we'll slip into the woods. Bring the blankets."

"But won't they just follow our footsteps in the snow and come after us?" Marshall asked.

"Not if we trick them," Dink said. "Let's all go out and make a lot of tracks going in five different directions. Really trample the snow up, all around the van. They won't know which way we went."

The kids stomped all over the snow, making it impossible for anyone to see a trail.

"Pick up branches for the fire!" Josh told everyone.

They came back to the fire and threw on whatever branches they'd found. Ruth Rose had stuffed her pockets with pinecones. They made a crackle as new flames shot up. The moonlight made the snow sparkle around them.

"I think they're coming. Listen!" Ruth Rose hissed.

They heard a *chug-chug*. They all looked toward the road.

"I see the plow's lights!" Dink said. "Let's go, and stay together!"

He led the others into the trees, all dragging their blankets. Soon they were hidden in shadows. Dink felt sure that Jo and the man she'd called Ace wouldn't be able to follow them.

The kids moved as quietly as possible. Dink pointed toward a giant pine tree. The lowest branches of the tree were half buried in snow.

"Under there," Dink whispered. He got down on his knees and forced himself between branches until he saw the tree's broad trunk. It was like being inside a hut. Dink had gotten sap all over his jacket and gloves. He tried getting rid of the stickiness by wiping it with snow.

The five kids crouched and waited. They were able to see the plow's lights and hear the engine. Dink tried, but he couldn't see Jo Payne or Ace. The engine noises stopped.

Minutes passed. Dink thought he heard shouting. Then the engine roared to life again. They all heard snow being moved and small trees snapping as they were crushed beneath the tires.

"He's burying the van!" Josh whispered in Dink's ear.

In less than five minutes, the van

had disappeared. The truck with the plow on the front made a clumsy turn and lumbered back up onto the road.

The kids waited. When several minutes had passed, they crept out from beneath the pine branches.

"Did . . . did they try to kill us by burying the van?" KC asked.

"No," Dink said. "They must have looked for us in the van and found it empty. They must think we ran away."

"What will they do now?" Ruth Rose asked. "They don't have Natasha anymore, and they don't have KC, either."

"I don't know," Dink said. "If they're smart, they'll disappear. Remember, we know their names and what Jo Payne looks like. And I saw Ace, too."

"Do you really want us to dig a tunnel into the van?" Josh asked.

Dink checked his watch. The moon made it easy to see in the dark.

"I think that's the safest place for now," he said. "It's almost eleven-thirty. Tomorrow we can walk into town. I heard Ace say there's one a few miles down the road."

"In which direction?" Ruth Rose asked. "The road goes both ways, so which way do we walk?"

"I don't know," Dink said. "Maybe we . . ."

"But what about Natasha?" KC asked. "What if she comes back and we're not here?"

The other four stared at KC. Dink thought they'd never see the dog again, but he wouldn't say so.

"You're right, KC," Dink said. "We wait for Natasha. Let's get busy digging."

"What do we use, our hands?" Marshall asked.

"Yeah, and break off some tree branches," Dink said.

Armed with broken branches, the kids approached the mound. Dead leaves, stones, and small trees were embedded in the snow. If Dink hadn't known better, he would have thought he was standing next to a huge, snow-covered boulder.

"How do we know where to dig?" Ruth Rose asked. "I mean, where are the van's rear doors?"

"On this end," Dink said. "Ace didn't move the van. He just covered it."

The five kids began picking at the mound with their branches. They soon discovered that chunks of ice were beneath the surface. This made their work even harder than they thought it would be.

When they came across sticks and branches, they tossed them into the fire, now nearly out again. After fifteen minutes of hacking away at snow and ice,

they'd only managed to remove two feet of the difficult snow.

"We need shovels," Josh said.

"You're right," Dink said. "Why don't you send a text message to your local hardware store and order a few for us."

"Okay, give me your cell phone," Josh said.

"I'd give a million dollars for a cell phone," Dink muttered. "Keep digging."

A half hour passed. They had created a cave. All five were in the cave, digging on their hands and knees.

"Guys, I think I hit the van!" Marshall cried.

They all began clawing wildly at the snow and ice with their hands, like five dogs digging in the sand.

"You're right!" Dink said. "It's the rear bumper!"

Suddenly they heard the roar of

engines. A strong beam of light lit their
snow cave. When they turned, the light
blinded them.

Dink backed out and stood up. He
put up a hand to keep the bright lights
from his eyes. He saw two snowmobiles
parked next to the weakly burning fire.

Dink swallowed. He felt his stomach
lurch into a knot. A man sat on one
of the snowmobiles. The other rider
looked like a woman. Ace and Jo.
They'd come back!

"Run!" Dink screamed.

CHAPTER 8

Josh, Ruth Rose, KC, and Marshall all tried to back out of the cave at the same time. They tripped over each other's feet as they tried to escape. The snow mobiles' headlights created frantic shadows on the snow.

Dink was knocked to the ground. He felt Josh crawling over him.

Then he heard a bark. Were they being attacked by wolves, too?

"Natasha!" KC cried. More barking.

Dink sat up. Natasha was lying on top of KC, covering her face with kisses. The dog's red sweater was caked with

ice and snow. As the other kids watched, Natasha stopped licking KC's face. The dog whimpered once, then rolled over into the snow.

"Something's the matter with her!" Marshall said, crawling over to KC.

The man and woman climbed off their snowmobiles. Dink realized that they were not Ace and Jo Payne after all. The man was too short, for one thing. And his voice sounded young when he said, "Your dog is awesome. She led us here from a mile away."

He was wearing some kind of padded snowsuit that zipped up the front. Ski goggles and a helmet covered most of his face. Only his eyes showed.

Dink, Josh, and Ruth Rose were kneeling in the snow next to Natasha, who wasn't moving. KC was stroking Natasha's icy fur and whispering in her ear.

"What's wrong with her?" KC asked.

"Probably hypothermia," the woman said. She was dressed like the man, in ski goggles and a helmet. Dink realized they were teenagers. "I'm Loren, and this is my brother, Tinker."

"Hypothermia can be pretty bad," her brother said. "One of my buddies got lost in the snow last year. It was real cold and he stayed out way too long. When he didn't come home, his folks called the cops. They found him asleep in a snowbank. His face was blue, and his temperature was way down. He almost died."

"Oh no!" KC cried.

"Don't worry," Tinker said. "We'll get your dog to our house. Mom knows a lot about animals. It'll be cool. Let's load her up on my snowmobile."

"We can take you all," Loren said. "But you'll have to sit on top of each

other. What're you kids doing out here, anyway?"

"It's a long story," Dink said.

"Cool, but tell us later," Tinker said. "Let's hit the road!"

Dink and KC wrapped Natasha in one of the packing blankets. Tinker carried the bundle to his snowmobile and held her on his lap. Dink, Josh, and KC scrunched together into the passenger section behind Tinker's seat. Marshall and Ruth Rose climbed on the other snowmobile behind Loren.

In moments, they were skimming over the snowy road. Dink's eyes blurred as they whipped past trees and snow-covered fields. The moonlight made everything seem like a dream.

Ten minutes later, Tinker aimed his snowmobile up a long, plowed driveway. At the end sat a small house. Dink smelled smoke from the chimney. Lights were on, glowing through the windows.

Tinker and Loren parked their snowmobiles near the porch and the kids jumped off. Tinker carried Natasha up the snowy front steps. A Christmas wreath hung on the door.

Loren opened the door and everyone clattered in.

"Boots off, you two!" a voice called from another room. "And you said you'd be home by eleven!"

Tinker kicked out of his boots, then laid Natasha on a rug in front of the

fireplace. Four stockings hung from the mantel. In the fireplace itself, a small wood fire crackled. Dink noticed a Christmas tree in one corner, with a few wrapped presents arranged on a red cloth.

"Mom, I have a surprise for you!" Tinker yelled toward the next room. He grinned at the others.

A tall woman stepped into the room. She was wearing jeans and a sweatshirt with a parrot on the front. She stopped when she saw five strange kids dripping snow onto her rug.

"Usually he brings me baby squirrels or orphaned birds," she said. "Who do we have here?"

The five wet, cold kids introduced themselves.

"We found them in a snowbank!" Loren said. "Their dog led us right to them!"

"What dog?" her mother asked.

Loren pointed to the blanket on the hearth.

Her mom knelt by the dog and carefully unwrapped the blanket. She forced Natasha's eyes open, then her mouth.

"Loren and Tinker, find some dry clothes for your friends." Loren followed her brother to the second floor.

"Will she be all right?" KC asked.

The woman sat back on her feet. "Yes, sweetie," she said. "Your dog's just exhausted and very cold. We'll have her fixed up in a jiffy."

She took a close look at the five kids. "Lordy, you all look like you've been through a war!" she said.

"We got kidnapped!" Marshall said.

"Wait, we want to hear!" Tinker said. He rushed into the room with an armful of sweatpants. Loren was right behind him. She dropped a pile of sweatshirts on the sofa.

"Okay, you kids all get into warm stuff now," Loren and Tinker's mother ordered. "Loren, why don't you make a pot of hot chocolate? Tinker, we need more firewood."

"Um, Mrs.—" Dink started to say.

"I'm Molly Makepeace," the woman said.

"Mrs. Makepeace, could we make a couple of phone calls?" Dink went on. "Our parents don't know where we are."

"Sure, sweetie," Molly Makepeace said. "Use the phone in the kitchen."

The five kids quickly pulled on too-large sweatshirts and pants. Dink and KC went to the kitchen to find the phone. "You first," Dink said, then he went back to wait in the living room.

Everyone was gathered around Natasha, who was sitting up and licking faces.

KC stepped into the room with the phone. "Um, my stepfather wants to know what town we're in."

"Tell him Maple Crossing, Virginia," Molly Makepeace said. "We're number fifteen Fox Run Drive."

KC repeated the address into the phone, then listened for a reply.

"He wants to know if there's a place to land a helicopter," KC said.

"Your dad has a helicopter?" Tinker said.

"There's a big field behind the house," Molly said. "Plenty of room to land there. Tell him we'll have lights on."

KC finished and hung up. "They'll be here in a half hour. He promised to call your father at the hotel," KC told Dink. "And your parents are at the White House already, Marshall."

Dink smiled. He could just see his dad chatting with the president.

"White House? Kidnapped?" Molly Makepeace said. "What's going on here?"

"Well, the president is—" KC started to say.

"Wait!" Loren said. "The hot chocolate. Don't say anything till I get back!"

Soon they all had mugs of hot chocolate. Natasha was sitting up against KC's knees.

"Okay, kids, tell us how you know the president," Molly Makepeace said.

"He's my stepfather," KC said. "Last year, he and my mom fell in love and got married."

"So you live in the . . . White House?" Loren asked.

KC grinned. "Yup."

"And you got kidnapped?" Tinker said. "All five of you?"

The kids kept interrupting each other as they told the whole story. Natasha perked up her ears when they got to the part about her being locked in the crate.

When they were finished, Molly and

the two teenagers just stared.

"That is the most amazing story I ever heard!" Molly said. "And you managed to get away from that man and woman. Do you know who they are?"

"Her name is Josephine Payne," Dink said. "I found papers in her glove compartment. And I heard her call him Ace. I think the guy lives near here."

"Ace Boyd!" Tinker yelled. "He's a total wacko! He and my dad got in a big fight when Ace tried to shoot some wild turkeys on our property."

"You know him?" Ruth Rose asked.

"Everybody around here knows Ace Boyd," Molly said. "But no one wants to know him. He manages to make enemies wherever he sets foot."

"I've seen him throwing his trash in our field," Loren said. "Ace Boyd belongs in jail!"

"I guess he and Jo Payne planned to

kidnap Natasha when Jo was hanging wreaths in the White House," Dink said.

"Yeah, and we went along for the ride," Josh added. "That's the last time I do anything nice for you, Natasha!" Josh gave the dog a big kiss on her head.

"How did you find her?" Marshall asked Tinker and Loren.

Tinker smiled. "Dude, your dog found us," he said. "Loren and I were out doing some night snowmobiling. It got too windy, so we decided to come back here. Next thing I know, this thing all covered in ice jumps in front of me. I almost fell off my snowmobile! I thought it was a grizzly bear come to eat me."

"She barked at us and kept backing away, like she was trying to say something," Loren said. "Finally we just followed her until we saw you guys."

KC gave Natasha a smooch. "You're

my heroine!" she said. "I'm going to make you some Christmas doggie cookies."

"Speaking of eating, when is the last time you five had a meal?" Molly asked.

"Yesterday!" Josh said.

"We ate around two o'clock in the afternoon," Ruth Rose said. "But our friend Josh is like a baby bird. He has to eat every five minutes."

"How do soup and sandwiches sound?" Molly asked, heading toward the kitchen. "And blueberry pie?"

"Can I come and live with you guys?" Josh asked.

CHAPTER 9

They ate in the kitchen.

"This table looks like a pack of wolves had a picnic here," Molly Makepeace said. The seven kids had devoured all the soup, a plateful of sandwiches, and a whole pie. Natasha lay under the table, waiting for something to fall her way.

"We saw wolves at the National Zoo," Dink said. "The puppies look just like dog puppies."

"We don't have any wolves here in Virginia anymore," Loren said.

"Really? I was sure I heard wolves

when we were stuck in that van!" Josh said.

"You probably heard coyotes," Tinker said. "My dad told me he sees coyotes around here all the time."

"Where is your dad?" Dink asked. He remembered the four stockings hanging above the fireplace.

"In the army," Loren said. "But he'll be home in time for Christmas."

"Yikes, what time is it?" Tinker said. He jumped up. "Come on, Loren, let's turn on our snowmobile lights. The president is coming!"

Everyone put on hats, coats, and boots. Molly found a leash for Natasha. "We don't want her running off again!" she said.

While Tinker and Loren started their snowmobiles, Molly found a few flashlights. Then she led the five kids out to a large, flat area behind the house. "In

the summer, this is a pick-your-own strawberry field," she said. "The kids run the business and save the profits for college."

Tinker and Loren came roaring around the corner on their snowmobiles. They made a giant circle in the snow, then pulled up and parked next to their mother and the five kids.

"Let's spread out around the circle," Dink said. He still had the flashlight he'd taken from the van. Molly handed out the other flashlights, and they each took a position.

Eight faces were turned toward the sky. The snowmobile lights threw their shadows into the circle.

Suddenly Natasha let out a bark. She pointed her muzzle up and began to whimper.

A moment later, they all heard what Natasha had heard.

"It's the helicopter!" Dink said. "Turn on the flashlights!"

A dark object flew in front of the moon. Tiny lights blinked on and off as the object flew lower in the sky.

"They see us!" Josh cried.

Everyone began waving their flashlights as the chopper came closer. Dink's hat almost blew off his head from the wind made by the blades.

Natasha began to howl. She tugged on her leash as the helicopter landed in the middle of the circle.

"She knows who it is," KC said.

They all stared at the black helicopter. Then a side door opened and the President of the United States stepped out.

"Oh my gosh," said Tinker. "It really *is* him!"

KC and Natasha ran toward the president.

After all the hugging was over, KC led her stepfather over to introduce him to her new friends.

Everyone shook hands with President Zachary Thornton.

He looked at Dink, Josh, and Ruth Rose. "I understand you stayed with KC and Marshall through the entire ordeal," he said. "Thank you very much. I owe you."

Dink blushed down to his toes. "Natasha was the real hero," he said. "She went to get help and led Tinker and Loren right to us."

"Did you fly that yourself . . . sir?" Tinker asked the president.

"No, I brought my pilot," the president said. "Jeff and I have been out looking since we found the note."

"What note?" KC asked.

"Your mom found it on one of the Christmas wreaths," the president told

her. "It was a ransom note for Natasha. A little while later, we realized you and Marshall were gone, too."

"Would you and your pilot like to come inside?" Molly asked. "The kids ate every scrap of food, but I could make coffee."

"That would be wonderful," the president said.

Twenty minutes later, everyone was crowded into the living room. The five kids were telling everyone how they burned the spare tire on the bonfire, when there was a knock on the door.

"More company?" Molly said. "It's way after midnight!"

"I think I know who it is," the president said. "I sent a couple of FBI boys to collect the bad guys."

Molly opened the door. Two big men in dark uniforms stood on the porch.

Between them were Jo Payne and Ace Boyd. The pair was handcuffed together.

The president looked at KC. "Are these the people who took you?" he asked.

"She is," KC said. "I never got a good look at him, though."

"I did!" Dink said. He pulled the cigarette from his pocket. "I was hiding ten feet away and I saw his face. He was smoking this."

"Thank you," the president said. He took the cigarette butt and slipped it into a pocket. "Agents Dirk and Lynch, take these two back to the city and lock them up. Have FBI Director Smiley call me tomorrow."

"Yes, sir!" The FBI agents and their prisoners left.

"We have to leave, too," the president said. "Molly, Tinker, and Loren, thank you for what you did. If there's anything I can ever do, please call me."

"The White House?" Tinker asked. "Like, just call you?"

The president smiled. "Yes, Tinker," he said. "Like, just call me."

The kids all hugged Molly and Tinker and Loren. Then Jeff the pilot helped the five kids and Natasha climb into the helicopter. When everyone was strapped in, he took the chopper up out of the Makepeaces' strawberry field.

Fifteen minutes later, Dink poked Josh and Ruth Rose. "Look," he said. He pointed down. They were flying over the White House.

Surrounded by snow and with all the lights on, the White House looked magical. Jeff landed the helicopter on the president's special landing pad.

Everyone thanked Jeff, then they all followed the president to his private residence. Dink was surprised to see his

father sitting on the sofa in the president's living room.

"Dad!" Dink said. "How'd you get here?"

"President Thornton was kind enough to send a car for me," Dink's father said. "Lois and Mr. and Mrs. Li and I have had a nice chat about how our kids manage to get in trouble."

"Dad, it wasn't our fault!" Dink said. "That crazy lady drove away while we were trying to rescue Natasha."

His father smiled. "I know that, son," he said.

Dink, Josh, and Ruth Rose were all introduced to KC's mom and Marshall's parents.

When everyone had found seats, KC's mom said, "What I don't understand is how this Jo Payne knew that Natasha was the president's dog."

"Mom, Natasha's sweater says FIRST

DOG on it," KC said. "You should know, you knitted it for her!"

Everyone had a good laugh.

"So I guess Jo Payne figured she could steal the dog and get some ransom money," Dink said.

"And the rest of us were just along for the ride," Josh said, rubbing his sore arm.

KC yawned. "The First Stepdaughter is tired," she said.

The president stood up. "I think we all need to get to bed," he said.

"I can't wait to get back to the hotel," Josh said.

"Actually, you and Dink and Marshall will be sharing Lincoln's bedroom tonight," the president said. He winked at Dink's father.

"We're sleeping here tonight?" Josh yelped. "In the White House?"

"Yes, everyone is having a sleepover,"

KC's mom said. "Ruth Rose, you can share KC's room."

"I brought our luggage," Dink's father told Dink, Josh, and Ruth Rose. "Your pajamas and things are already in your rooms."

"Mr. Li and I will head home," Marshall's mother said. "I have to be up early for work." She kissed Marshall. "Get some sleep, and no staying up all night talking."

The kids all shared a high five.

• • •

Later, just as Dink was falling asleep, Josh poked him.

"What?" Dink asked.

"I heard something funny," Josh said.

"Josh, it's almost two in the morning," Dink said. "I don't want to hear any of your lame jokes."

"I heard something weird," Josh insisted. "A voice out in the hall."

Marshall was sleeping on the sofa. "What's going on?" he asked, sitting up.

"Josh is hearing things," Dink said.

"I'm not hearing things!" Josh said. "Someone is out there!"

"And I know who it is," Marshall whispered. "It's KC pulling her Lincoln's ghost joke again."

"I'll bet Ruth Rose put her up to it!" Josh said.

Marshall slipped off the sofa and wrapped his sheet around himself. "Get

your sheets and follow me," he whispered to Dink and Josh.

Marshall led the two boys to a small door behind the sofa.

"Where does this go?" Dink asked.

"You'll see."

They entered a bathroom. Marshall pointed to a tall cupboard near the bathtub. "It leads to a secret passageway."

He opened the cupboard, revealing a hallway. At the end was another door. "That goes to the main hall," he whispered. "Don't let the girls see us."

Marshall opened the door as quietly as he could. He stuck his head out, then motioned to Dink and Josh.

The boys saw two figures covered in sheets. They were crouched outside the door to the Lincoln Bedroom.

Dink saw Ruth Rose's red sneakers sticking out from under one of the sheets.

"Let's get 'em!" Marshall whispered. "Cover up."

The three boys draped the sheets over their heads, leaving room to see where they were walking. They crept up behind the girls, waving their arms like flying ghosts.

"Good evening," Josh said in his deepest, spookiest voice.

The two crouching figures jumped up. Ruth Rose screamed. KC shoved open the door to the Lincoln Bedroom and they both ran in.

Dink, Josh, and Marshall went right in behind them, still waving their arms in the air and making ghost noises.

"I know it's you, Marshall Li!" KC said, whipping off her sheet.

"And I recognized your voice, Joshua," Ruth Rose said. She yanked off her sheet.

"Gotcha!" Josh said.

They all started to laugh.

Dink heard knocking be
and turned around.

A tall man wearing a black suit stood in the doorway. He had a black beard and a tall black hat on his head.

The five kids froze as if turned to ice.

Dink gulped. He could hardly swallow. He was staring at the ghost of Abraham Lincoln!

"I hope you enjoy sleeping in my room," the figure of Abe Lincoln said. "Don't forget to make the bed tomorrow. Good night."

The man closed the door and walked away.

As the man walked down the hall, he heard screaming from the room behind him. Smiling, he pulled off the fake beard and top hat.

"Boy, I love doing that," President Zachary Thornton said to himself.

DID YOU FIND THE
SECRET MESSAGE
HIDDEN IN THIS BOOK?

If you *don't* want
to know the answer,
don't look at the bottom
of this page!

Answer:
THE GHOST OF LINCOLN ROAMS FREE

HAVE YOU READ ALL THE BOOKS IN THE

A to Z Mysteries® SERIES?

Help Dink, Josh, and Ruth Rose . . .

A to Z Mysteries

THE MISSING MUMMY
by Ron Roy

THE NINTH NUGGET
by Ron Roy

THE ORANGE OUTLAW
by Ron Roy

THE PANDA PUZZLE
by Ron Roy

The Panda Paper
Baby Panda STOLEN!

THE QUICKSAND QUESTION

THE RUNAWAY RACEHORSE
by Ron Roy

THE SCHOOL SKELETON
by Ron Roy

THE TALKING T. REX

THE UNWILLING UMPIRE
by Ron Roy

THE VAMPIRE'S VACATION
by Ron Roy

THE WHITE WOLF
by Ron Roy

THE RED-OUT X-RAY
by Ron Roy

THE YELLOW YACHT
by Ron Roy

THE ZOMBIE ZONE
by Ron Roy

...solve
mysteries
from A to Z!

Collect clues with
Dink, Josh, and Ruth Rose
in their next exciting adventure

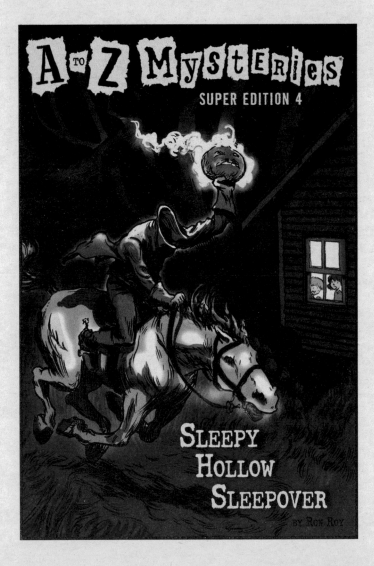

SLEEPY HOLLOW SLEEPOVER

"I saw a light," Dink whispered. "It was moving through the trees."

Josh gasped.

A horse raced out of the trees, past the cabin window. A rider carrying a jack-o'-lantern sat on the horse's back. The horse stopped, and the rider held the jack-o'-lantern high in the air.

"What on earth is anyone doing riding around in the dark?" Dink's father asked.

Dink noticed the rider's flowing cloak. Then he looked above the man's shoulders. There was nothing there.

"I think he's looking for his head," Dink whispered.

"IT'S THE HEADLESS HORSEMAN!" Ruth Rose screamed in Josh's ear.

A to Z Mysteries® fans, check out Ron Roy's other great mystery series!

Capital Mysteries

#1: Who Cloned the President?
#2: Kidnapped at the Capital
#3: The Skeleton in the Smithsonian
#4: A Spy in the White House
#5: Who Broke Lincoln's Thumb?
#6: Fireworks at the FBI
#7: Trouble at the Treasury
#8: Mystery at the Washington Monument
#9: A Thief at the National Zoo
#10: The Election-Day Disaster
#11: The Secret at Jefferson's Mansion
#12: The Ghost at Camp David
#13: Trapped on the D.C. Train!
#14: Turkey Trouble on the National Mall

January Joker
February Friend
March Mischief
April Adventure
May Magic
June Jam
July Jitters
August Acrobat
September Sneakers
October Ogre
November Night
December Dog
New Year's Eve Thieves

If you like **A TO Z MYSTERIES**®, take a swing at

BALLPARK Mysteries®

#1: The Fenway Foul-Up

#2: The Pinstripe Ghost

#3: The L.A. Dodger

#4: The Astro Outlaw

#5: The All-Star Joker

#6: The Wrigley Riddle

#7: The San Francisco Splash

#8: The Missing Marlin

#9: The Philly Fake

#10: The Rookie Blue Jay

#11: The Tiger Troubles

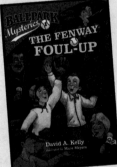